# SPIDERS

# SPIDERS

## *Alice L. Hopf*
### *Photographs by Ann Moreton*

COBBLEHILL BOOKS
*Dutton • New York*

## *Acknowledgment*

We wish to thank Professor Herbert W. Levi of the Museum of Comparative Zoology at Harvard University for checking the manuscript and photographs for accuracy.

Library of Congress Cataloging-in-Publication Data
Hopf, Alice Lightner, 1904 –
Spiders / Alice L. Hopf ; photographs by Ann Moreton.
P.      cm.
Includes index.
Summary: Describes, in text and photographs, the physical characteristics, habits, and natural environment of a variety of spiders.
ISBN 0-525-65017-2
1. Spiders—Juvenile literature.   [1. Spiders.]   I. Moreton, Ann, ill.   II. Title.
QL458.4.H66 1990
595.4'.4—dc20          89-9716
CIP   AC

Published in the United States by E.P. Dutton,
New York, N.Y., a division of Penguin Books USA Inc.
Published simultaneously in Canada by
Fitzhenry and Whiteside Limited, Toronto
Designed by Jean Krulis
Printed in Hong Kong
First edition   10 9 8 7 6 5 4 3 2 1

# CONTENTS

# 1

## *An Infinite Variety*

Many people think of spiders as insects, but they are not. Insects have six legs while spiders have eight. Other big differences are that insects may have wings and some feed on vegetation, while spiders never have wings and all are meat-eaters. Spiders feed mostly on insects and in doing so are very helpful. They keep down the large populations of insects that destroy our crops, spread disease, and are generally pests.

People also think of spiders as web-spinners. All spiders make silk, but only certain species use it to catch insects with webs. Silk has always been used in the most important construction in the

spider's life: the protection of the next generation. It is used to make the egg sac in which the female lays her eggs. There the babies grow until they are big enough to care for themselves.

Spiders are very numerous. There are some 35,000 species worldwide, and new ones are being discovered all the time. Scientists working in the rain forests of Panama have estimated that there are about 264,000 spiders per acre in the forest floor.

Scientists place spiders in a group of animals called Arachnida. The name comes from Greek mythology and a story about a Greek maiden called Arachne. She was the champion weaver of her village and so proud of her work that she challenged the goddess Athena to a contest. When the goddess saw what Arachne could do, she was very jealous and angry. She changed poor Arachne into a spider!

The Arachnida are creatures with four pairs of legs and only two body parts: a combined head and chest area, the *cephalothorax*, and an abdomen. (Insects have three body parts.) The cephalothorax has a hard, protective outer covering called the *carapace*. The two parts of the body are connected by a thin stalk, the *pedicel*. Each of the spider's eight legs has seven parts with joints and if it should lose a leg, a spider can grow a new one. The spider also has eight eyes; some are large, others may be small. They are arranged across its head in various patterns that may help tell the family to which it belongs—if a jumper or an orb-weaver. Some exceptions are the few species that have only six . . . or four . . . or

A golden garden spider, hanging head down on an incomplete web.

two eyes. And then there are spiders that live in the total darkness of caves and have no eyes at all.

The jaws (*chelicerae*) are in front of the head. They are tipped with fangs that have poison duct openings near the ends. Between the jaws and the first legs are leglike appendages, small in females but larger in the males, with swollen tips. The tips are called *palps* or *palpi* and are used by the males when mating.

Spiders liquify their food before it is sucked into their mouths. Some spiders pump digestive juices into their victims and then suck juices from them. Others chew the insects into a ball mixed with digestive juices. They cover the prey with their own digestive juices, and the edible parts are turned into a kind of "soup" which the spiders suck up. When finished, there is only a dry shell or a small hard lump of material left.

Spiders have no bones, no internal skeletons to hold their bodies together. That is taken care of by the tough outer skin. But as the spider grows, its skin becomes too small for it. The spider sheds the tight skin and a new skin emerges underneath. This process is called molting. It may take several hours and is a difficult and dangerous time for a spider. The spider cannot defend itself and is open to attack from its many enemies while its new skin is still soft.

Spiders are famous for their silken webs which they use in

A small stick was used to touch the spinnerets as the spider hung in her web. The spider released her silk, which was drawn out and wrapped around the stick.

many ways. The silk emerges from tiny tubes on the spinnerets. The spinnerets—usually six—are located at the end of the abdomen. The silk emerges from the tubes in liquid form, but hardens as it is pulled from the spinnerets. The spider can control the kind of silk it uses: sticky or nonsticky, according to need. Different silk is used for safety lines, for attaching silk to the surface, for egg sacs, and several different kinds for webs.

# 2

## *The Web-Weavers*

Only about half of the kinds of spiders use their silk to trap insects. It is not known just when the spiders developed this ability. Scientists learn the ancient history of animals and plants from fossils in the rocks, and anything as fragile as a spider does not leave many fossils. The earliest spider fossils are found in the coal beds of the Carboniferous era, and by that time spiders were already spinning webs. We can only guess at what may have influenced those early spiders to begin to use their silk for trapping prey.

Spiders can wait a long time between meals. Sometimes over a month, if necessary. But they always need water. So it may have been easier for an early spider just to sit and wait for the prey to come to it, rather than to run after it, as the hunting spiders still do today. And while sitting and waiting, the result can be more certain if there is a trap prepared for the prey.

There are many different forms of web traps, each used by a different species of spider. Each web-weaving species has its own special web and spinning it is instinctive. A spider does not "think" about spinning a web and does not have to learn to do so. It does it automatically. If it is interrupted in its work, it may have to start all over again with step one. When the work is finished, the spider may hang quietly in its web, or it may go to a spot nearby to hide. Some spiders have lines of silk that run from the webs to their hiding places. By holding onto this line, a spider feels any vibration in the web and knows at once when an insect has been caught. The spider then hurries to claim its prize.

If the victim is a small insect, the spider will rush right down and bite it with its poison fangs. Then it will feed on it or wrap it in silk and hang it up in the web for a later meal. If the captive is a large insect, perhaps with a poison sting like a bee or a wasp, the spider may wrap it first or hesitate. (Most orb-weaving spiders wrap most large prey first before biting, but not slippery moths.) Sometimes the spider can get hold of an insect leg where the victim cannot reach it and inject its own poison. But if the insect is too large, it may cut it loose.

There is a great variety of web traps in the spider world. Some might seem unimportant to us, like the small bluish blobs of webbing sometimes found around doors and window ledges, in cellars and sheds.

A marbled orb-web spinner (*Araneus marmoreus*) outside its retreat.
One foot rests lightly on a trap line.

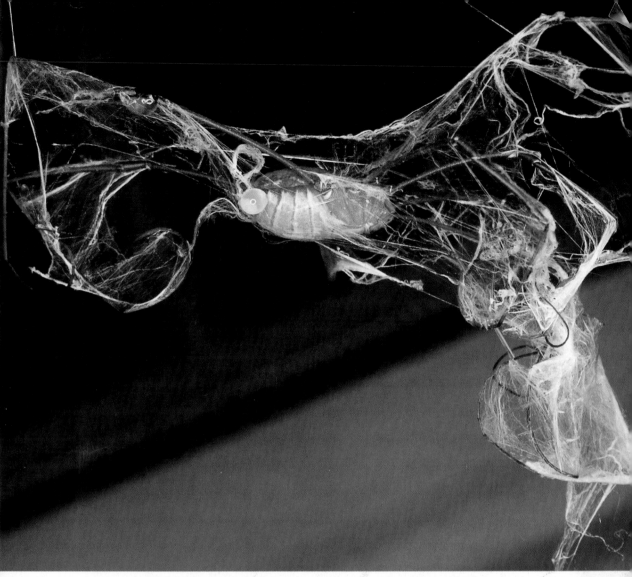

A spider uses silk to subdue prey according to the mass of the prey on the web. A daddy longlegs only requires a thin covering of silk; wide bands of silk are used for heavy prey such as grasshoppers.

An orb-web spinner capturing a wasp. She runs close to the wasp and flings silk over a leg, securing it. This is repeated in cautious dashes back and forth above the wasp.

Another group of spiders (*Theridion*) leaves its silk threads extending in all directions, crossing and recrossing in a kind of maze. The spiders are small, brightly colored creatures that make their webs in bushes and hedges, or under stones.

Members of the genus *Linyphia* are sometimes called hammock makers. Their silk is so fine that the "hammocks" spread across shrubs and hedges, looking like misty clouds. The spider sits just below, waiting for insects to fly against a thread and fall into the web to be trapped.

The genus *Agelenopsis* makes webs similar to those of hammock spiders, with a funnel hole on the side of the retreat of the spider. They are found on lawns, on the bases of bushes, and in corners of windows.

The genus *Araneus* includes the spiders that make the well-known orb webs, of cartwheel design. The best-known orb-weaver is the *Argiope*, easily seen and observed in our gardens. Anyone watching this spider make its web will be impressed by the exact measurements and the overall beauty of the final results.

The frame and spokes are made of nonsticky silk; the lines going all around are sticky. Orb webs are designed to catch flying insects, so the spider constructs a spiral. It begins at the center, where all the radii join, goes round and round, moving outward. Then as it spirals back inward, the spider switches to sticky silk.

The dome spider, *Linyphia marginata*, spins her web in bushes, in high grass, and in trees, especially pines. The spider lives inside the dome and catches insects that strike the web.

As each bit of sticky thread is pulled out of its spinnerets, it is fastened to a radius, which is then pulled taut with the spider's leg. Both sticky globules and nonsticky lines are made of silk. The spider spins this part, called the hub, in closer and denser circles. No insect can get through it. The hub is usually not made with sticky silk. At the very center, the spider may bite a hole in the hub. Some spiders rest in the hub, hanging head downward waiting for prey. Other spiders may hide in the foliage beyond the web, holding onto a signal thread, whose vibrations will tell it when a victim has been caught.

Some webs are decorated with broad zigzag lines of shining white silk, which scientists call *stabilimentum*. It once was thought that this extra webbing served to strengthen the web or perhaps to hide the spider. But recently, experiments done in the United States have proven that the purpose is to show up the almost invisible web to large flying creatures like birds and prevent them from ruining the structure and getting entangled.

Another quite elaborate web, designed to catch insects walking on the forest floor, is made by spiders of the family Theridiidae. They are small, globular-shaped spiders. (The black widow is one of this group.) This kind of spider builds a web of scaffoldlike

Inset: Funnel-web spiders spin webs in convenient openings. The webs are found in grass and ivy, on shrubs and logs. The spider lives in the funnel part of the web, with sometimes only her front feet visible.

Sparkling with dew, an orb web hangs on a weed.

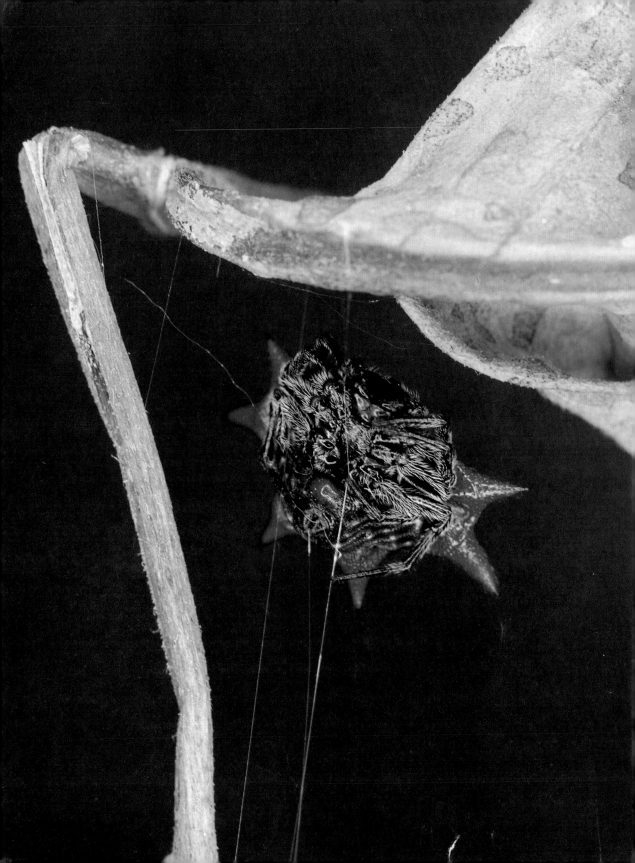

threads in the vegetation above an open spot. The spider hangs in its web. As each thread is attached to the ground by the spider, the bottom of the thread is coated with sticky globules. When an insect blunders into one of these lines, it gets stuck to the sticky threads. As it struggles to get free, it pulls the line loose from the ground and the spider's silk, which is elastic and has been pulled tightly, springs upward, carrying the victim off the ground. The spider feels the vibrations in its web, rushes to the proper line, and hauls in the victim.

Left: An orb spinner (*Gasteracantha cancriformis*) is found in Florida, stringing support lines.

A young *Argiope* spins great quantities of silk in the hub of the web.

# 3

## *The Hunters*

About half of all spiders catch their prey without webs. They hunt to obtain their food. Some of them have invented unusual ways of using their silk to catch prey.

There are a great many wolf spiders (Lycosidae), some large and some small. They are called wolf spiders because, like wolves, they run down their prey. But the likeness ends there. Wolves are social animals and hunt in packs. Wolf spiders are solitary creatures and live alone.

Wolf spiders are well equipped to chase their victims. They have long legs and good eyesight, for spiders. The eight eyes are set close together on the front part of the face. They have strong jaws to crush their prey, once it is captured.

Wolf spiders are found all over the world and are especially fond of open areas, where they can chase small insects among grasses. Others live in sandy areas, where they dig tunnels for protection and come out at night to catch small insects. They have even adapted to water environments and such species run on the surface. They can skate across the surface in pursuit of prey and even dive, if threatened by danger.

Although the female wolf spider is a hunter preying even on small spiders, she takes care of her young. All female spiders make egg sacs in which they lay their eggs. Most simply hang the sac up on nearby vegetation and then forget about it. But wolf spiders do not. Often the egg sac is as big as she is, but she carries it everywhere and will defend it with her life. When the eggs inside the sac have hatched and the babies have molted for the first time and are ready to come out, she tears open the sac and frees them.

Then the little spiderlings scramble upon her back and she carries them everywhere. They do not need to eat until they have molted again, but they do drink. When the mother stops by some water to quench her thirst, the spiderlings have been seen to climb down her legs and drink also. They do not leave her until after they have molted and are big enough to care for themselves.

Some species of wolf spiders dig burrows in soft or sandy soil and line them with silk. Here they hide from enemies and rush out to attack passing prey. They use their silk in building the burrows, lining the sides of their dens with it, and even using the

silk in the excavation. They cover little pellets of sand with silk which they carry out of the burrows and drop short distances away. Around the burrow openings they sometimes build little turrets of earth where they can sit and watch for prey. Some also construct doors to close the openings of their tunnels, much like those of trapdoor spiders.

Mating usually takes place outside the burrow and the male must persuade the female to come out. Once she has laid her eggs and made the sac, the burrowing wolf spider carries her sac with her, dragging it in and out of the burrow. Sometimes she sits in the mouth of the burrow and turns the egg sac over and over in the sun so that all parts will feel the warmth. Although the babies of most wolf spiders may leave their mothers a few weeks after hatching, those of the burrowing wolf spiders stay much longer, sometimes even all winter, in the burrows.

Another large group of hunting spiders is known as the jumping spiders. These spiders hunt more like cats than like wolves. The jumping spider waits until it has selected a special victim and then leaps on it from a fair distance. Jumping spiders have even better eyesight than the wolf spiders. Their large eyes allow them to see movement ahead of them and they creep up on the prey until near enough to perform one of their remarkable jumps.

The jumping spiders (Salticidae) are mostly small with short bodies and legs. Surprisingly, their hind legs, which do the jumping, are not much longer than their other legs. Probably the very

Wolf spiders carry their babies on their backs for about two weeks.

This *Phidippus* jumping spider was found under a picnic table in Kansas.

light weight of a spider makes such adaptations as we see in the grasshoppers and kangaroos unnecessary. The jumping spiders can leap up to forty times the length of their bodies.

Jumping spiders are some of the most colorful and most handsome spiders. The bodies are covered with thick hair or scales, often brightly colored, and the males may have spines and fringes of hair decorating their legs and bodies. These seem to hold the females' attention when used in the courting dances.

Like most spiders, the jumper lets out a dragline of silk behind it which can save it if it fails. Perhaps this accounts for the abandon with which it leaps after prey. The jumping spider has been seen to leap away from the side of a building to catch an insect in flight. Jumping spiders live all over the world, but the greatest varieties are in the tropics. One jumping spider was found 22,000 feet up on the slopes of Mount Everest, where few creatures of any sort can exist.

Some jumping spiders use their silk to spin a kind of protective tent under stones or plants or the bark of trees. There they hide when not hunting and may even spend the winter under the thick, white webbing. Here the female lays her eggs and stands guard over the young spiders. Sometimes a group of these little "tents" may be found under the same stone.

Another large group of hunting spiders is known as the crab spiders (Thomisidae). They are so named from their peculiar way of walking: sideways and backwards, much like crabs. They are not as lively as wolf spiders or jumping spiders. Like the web-weavers, they prefer to sit and let their prey come to them. But they do not use their silk to make traps. Instead, they rely on camouflage. Camouflage works in two ways. It protects the spider from its enemies and it hides it from the creature it is trying to catch.

A white crab spider on a yellow daisy, caught a hover fly on the flower. The spider grabbed it with her strong front legs and fangs delivered the poison.

This picture shows the two color phases of a crab spider (*Misumenoides aleatorius*).

Crab spiders are beautifully colored to match the flowers they sit on: pink or white or yellow. They seem to pick flowers of their own colors, but they can also change colors to match the flowers. However, a color change may take several days. Many insects come to flowers seeking nectar, which makes flowering plants good hunting grounds for the crab spiders.

The crab spider's camouflage goes beyond the matching of color. Some species manage to look like a variety of objects in the environment: the bark of trees, leaf buds, or dried seeds.

# 4

## *Mating*

For the male spider, mating is usually a dangerous adventure. In most species, the female is larger than the male. She may have poor eyesight and he has to make her recognize him as a mate, or she may decide that he is just the meal she has been waiting for and will eat him.

When a male spider is ready to mate, he must find a female. The male follows a silk thread. It can tell if it is made by a female waiting for a mate. The sense used is probably smell. Each species has its own way of courting a mate. Since they must be careful to keep their mates from eating them, the males must be sure the females know who they are and must also prepare for hurried escapes.

Among the web-weavers, the male usually signals his presence by plucking on the web, producing a vibration different from that caused by prey. If the female appears too aggressive, the male will let himself down from the web on an escape line.

The male spider is persistent and soon he will climb back up

The male moves above the female and waits a few seconds. The sperm is transferred into the openings on the female's abdomen.

his lifeline and again start tweaking on the web. He uses a leg to pull regularly and rhythmically—a kind of signal. The female recognizes the meaning of these vibrations, for she comes out again and slowly he approaches her. There is a great variation in the courting behavior of different spiders. The beautiful *Argiope* female may be more aggressive and dangerous. The male must approach her with great care. However, as he is smaller and more agile than she is, he usually manages to escape. But his work is done and he may die soon after mating. One female European spider that makes a flat sheet web is more cooperative. As soon as the male signals by pulling at her web, she folds her legs and falls over as though paralyzed and lets him drag her off to a convenient spot on the web where the mating takes place. Another male spider has the habit of taking a gift to his mate—an insect wrapped in silk. He can mate while she is eating.

The hunting spider males also follow silk lines of females. These spiders have better eyesight than the web spiders. Once the male is sure of his mate, he begins to signal to her. A wolf spider usually has decorative spines or hairs on its front legs. It waves these in the air before the female it is courting. One leg will point up and the other down. Then he will reverse the arrangement, all the while vibrating his body and his front legs. If the female has mated already and does not want to mate again, she may lunge at him and he must jump quickly away. But if she likes his looks, she will vibrate her body and mating will proceed. Some wolf spiders make sounds to attract the female, thumbing their bodies across dry leaves, or clicking legs. This has earned the males the name of "purring spiders."

A wolf spider in a courtship display.

The jumping spiders have perhaps the most unusual courting rituals. Not only are the males brightly colored, but they perform bizarre dances to catch the attention of females. As well as signaling with the palps, they also jump sideways and up and down. Each species has a different courting dance.

# 5

## *Motherhood*

When the spider's courting and mating rituals have been performed, the male goes on his own way and dies soon after. The female now has complete responsibility for the next generation. All female spiders lay eggs—from a few to a thousand—and wrap them up with silk in egg sacs.

To make her egg sac, the female first spins a flat sheet of silk. Usually oval, it is thick and dense. She then stands over it and lays a quantity of eggs. Egg laying takes only a minute or two, but the making of the sac takes longer. When the eggs are all there and the top sheet has been spun, the spider sews the two pieces to-

This spider is laying her eggs on a silken platform above the spider.

gether. Finally she takes hold of the egg sac and turns it about, at the same time putting down thick strands of silk so that soon the entire mass is well wrapped in a protective covering. She may add some pats and punches to make it more round and globular.

In general, this is the way spiders lay their eggs. But what happens now depends on the species and its habits. Many web-weaving spiders in the temperate zone live only one season and die with the first frost. By that time, the mother will have laid all her eggs, often making several egg sacs, which she hangs up in the web or attaches to some foliage nearby. The eggs do not hatch until the next spring and the spiderlings are left to manage on their own. Other spiderlings hatch in fall and overwinter as little spiders.

Things are quite different with the hunting, ground-dwelling spiders. Once these mothers have spun their egg sacs and laid their eggs, they carry the large bundles with them. Wolf spiders fasten them to the spinnerets at the ends of their abdomens. Other spiders may carry the egg sacs in their jaws, in which case, of course, they cannot eat or hunt.

Spiders that live in burrows may hang their egg sacs from the inner walls, where they will be protected from the cold and from enemies. Many insects hunt for spider egg sacs. Parasitic wasps and flies lay their eggs on them. The insect eggs hatch first and devour the spider eggs.

Some spiders that hide their sacs in burrows bring them regularly to the surface and turn the sacs over in the rays of the sun. This prevents the development of mold. The sheet-web spider spins a labyrinth of silk in which she hides her egg sac. Another spider

The egg sac of the green lynx spider, *Peucetia viridans*, is a bundle of pale brown and tufted silk. The spider ties the egg sac to vegetation and guards it until the young hatch.

that hangs her sac on a bush or tree has a habit of covering it with mud. One wolf spider that lives near water has been seen to dip its egg sac in the water, thus keeping the eggs from drying out. Other spiders spin long necks for the sacs so that they hang below the branches where they are fastened. This may have some protective value, discouraging ants and other predators from venturing down the long, thin lines.

Cold weather makes the little spiderlings inactive and they often overwinter inside the sac. They may also go through their first molt there. If the mother is still alive when it is time for the babies to leave the sac, she may help them by tearing a hole in it. But if she has died, the spiderlings are left to their own devices. A few of the most energetic will bite little holes in the sac and escape, and one by one the rest of the brood will squeeze out after them.

Now there will be hundreds of baby spiders, all looking for a home, a place to hide from predators. And predators turn up in abundance. How can the spiderlings all find shelter here? Spiders have a solution to this problem, and it is all done by instinct. For a while they cluster together in a web, if available, then they disperse.

Many baby spiders climb up anything around them—blades of grass, stems of plants, trunks of trees. Anything to get up where the breezes blow, for the spiderlings will go ballooning! Even some small-sized adults that are not too heavy do this. When the baby spider has climbed as high as it can, it raises its abdomen in the air and lets out a strand of silk. It may have to do this a number of times before the silk is caught by a breeze and pulls upward.

The delicate sheet web thrown across the grass. The tiny red spider (*Florinda coccinea*) darts away at the slightest disturbance.

When the spider feels the tug on the silk, it lets go its hold on the leaf and is carried away into the sky. Some may go only a short distance before the breeze fails and they drift back to earth. But some may travel a long way. Charles Darwin noted such an event when his ship, the *Beagle*, was sixty miles off the coast of Argentina. A swarm of little spiders, drifting on their strands of silk, came down upon the ship's deck. Later they all took off again and vanished over the water.

Spiders have been caught from airplanes in the air at 10,000 feet. The largest spiders, the ground-dwelling "tarantulas" and trapdoor spiders, do not go ballooning. They are too big and heavy to be carried aloft on a breeze.

Five miles of ballooning silk photographed in Slidell, Louisiana. Strong winds pulled the silk from the spider's bodies. When the wind ceased, the silk floated to earth. Photograph by Raiford Holmes.

# 6

## *The Biggest Spiders*

The name "tarantula" is misleading. It has been given to many different spiders, causing considerable confusion. It all began in Europe during the Middle Ages, when peasants living near the city of Taranto in Italy took part in wild, energetic dances. The authorities felt that such dancing was not proper, and they passed laws against it. The peasants, deprived of their favorite recreation, invented a story. One man would claim he had been bitten by a deadly spider and that the only remedy was to dance wildly until the poison wore off. Some even claimed that the spider's bite brought on the wild leaps and convulsions. The spider in question,

A red-kneed tarantula and molted skin.

a fairly large wolf spider, not at all poisonous to humans, became known as the tarantula. The dance is called the tarantella.

After Columbus discovered America and the Spaniards conquered and settled in South America, colonists in North America found large spiders. They were much, much bigger than the spiders in Europe and their legs and bodies were covered with long hairs. A very frightening sight! The colonists called them tarantulas—the most frightening name they knew for spiders. There are about 500 kinds of tarantulas. None in North America is poisonous. There are poisonous ones in South America and in Africa. All American "tarantulas" have hair with barbs on their abdomens. When handled they break off, or the spiders may throw them in defense. They cause a rash on the skin.

Tarantulas may make dense webs and use their silk for lining their nests. Some dig holes with their fangs and sometimes make little packets of dirt, rolled up in their silk, and carry them out of the burrows. Some species are arboreal, living in tree holes and hunting in trees.

Some spiders related to American tarantulas, known as trapdoor spiders, make doors that can open and close above their tunnels. The door is cemented together with dirt, saliva, and webbing. It even has a hinge, made by extending the silk from the wall lining into the door and fastening it all together with webbing.

Tarantulas live long lives for spiders. A female of one of the

Close-up photograph of a tarantula's fangs.

larger species can live up to twenty-five years. Males die much younger. Tarantulas may take from three to ten years to mature, depending on the species.

In the years before the Second World War there was a female tarantula living in the British Museum of Natural History in London. She had arrived in a bunch of bananas from South America, and when found was delivered alive to the museum. Her age was then estimated at six years and she became quite tame, and took food from people's fingers. She lived there for fourteen years. But then the war came. The museum had always been kept suitably warm, but because of fuel shortages heat was turned off at night. The spider froze to death. It is said that some tears were shed over her.

Although spiders are predators and kill large numbers of insects, they are also preyed upon by larger creatures. Birds may eat small spiders and spiderlings. Mammals like skunks, moles, and shrews may eat bigger ones. A female wasp may stuff a dozen little spiders after stinging them into the nest she is preparing for her offspring. Although each spider has been paralyzed by the wasp's sting, it is still alive. Thus the baby wasp, when it hatches from the egg, has enough food to last until it grows to the pupal stage and later emerges as an adult wasp.

There is one wasp, called *Pepsis*, that preys exclusively on big tarantula spiders. When the two meet there is a battle to the death, which the wasp usually wins.

As a defense against mammals, the tarantula sometimes scrapes loose some special hairs from its abdomen, which rise in a fine mist and upon contact with the skin or eyes of the attacker can

A trap-door spider is equipped with spiny rakes in its jaws, which are used to dig the tube burrow. The tube is lined with silk, including the door.

cause pain and itching. On the other hand, some of the largest tarantulas from South America have been known to capture and eat small birds and mice. Because of this, they are known as the "bird-eating spiders."

The largest tarantulas live in the rain forests of South America. They have given up the habit of digging burrows, for their homes could quickly be flooded. They even live in trees. Tarantulas are good climbers, as they have adhesive hairs on their feet.

Male tarantulas seldom live longer than the year in which they become adult. But the female has a long life ahead of her. By the time she has mated, she will have dug a large, comfortable burrow with plenty of room at the bottom where she can construct her egg sac. Like all spiders, she is very protective of her sac, which may hold as many as a hundred eggs. She watches over it, sometimes pulling it up to the mouth of the burrow to be warmed by the sun and then carrying it carefully down again. The eggs hatch in a few weeks, but the spiderlings stay in the sac for several more. Then they bite little holes in the webbing and climb out one by one.

In time all the spiderlings leave the burrow. They walk a few yards from the burrow and then dig their own homes. To begin with, these homes are very small, but as the spiderlings grow, they enlarge them. Tarantulas tend to live in colonies, which might be dangerous for them, as all spiders are cannibalistic. However, the tarantula's eyesight is so poor that it sees only light and dark. But the threads of other spiders and perhaps their smell or vibrations may make it aware of its neighbors.

# 7

## *Poisonous Spiders*

People are usually impressed by bigness. The bigger the better. Also the bigger the more dangerous. Today, the big American tarantulas cause terror to the ignorant. Because they are big and look scary, it is presumed that they must be aggressive and poisonous. Most of these spiders are not deadly to humans and they run and hide at the slightest disturbance.

However, there are poisonous spiders in America. In fact, there are several. There are black widows that hang in webs and will not readily leave the webs. The brown recluse may be aggressive, but the black widow has venom that is fifteen times more potent than an equal amount of that of the rattlesnake. The big difference is that the amount of venom that the spider can deliver is only a fraction of that carried by the snake. People rarely die from the bite of a black widow. The bite produces intense pain in the lower abdomen. Fortunately, there is an antivenin against the black widow's bite available, and anyone who is bitten should see a physician at once. With proper treatment, the patient should be well in a day or two.

The widows (*Latrodectus* sp.) are web-weaving spiders. There are several species in North America, most common the black widow *L. mactans* found in webs in trash in the Southeast. The male is much smaller than the female and does not bite. He presents no danger to humans. The spider gets its name from the mistaken belief that the female always eats the male after mating. This only happens occasionally, for the little male seems to be aware of his danger. He may throw some strands of silk across the female to help him escape when mating is finished. But the male may die while mating or soon after.

The black widow is often found in and around human dwellings. It makes its web in the crevices of old lumber piles or in outdoor toilets. Such outhouses are not often used today, but anyone venturing into one would do well to look under the seat before sitting down. This spider is small, globular, inky black, with long legs and a red hourglass marking on the underside.

The effect of a spider's bite can vary according to the individual bitten. Very small children and the elderly are the most apt to be badly affected. Also some people are more sensitive to bites than

A black widow (*Latrodectus mactans*) with egg sac. Hanging upside down in a tangled web, the red hourglass is very visible.

others. And finally it may depend on how much venom is injected. If the spider has just killed and eaten an insect, she may have used up most of her venom.

Like the widow spiders, the brown recluse (*Loxosceles reclusa*) makes its home near people. It spins a little web in cracks and crevices near sheds and outhouses. People working around such places may accidentally finger one of these spiders and receive a bite.

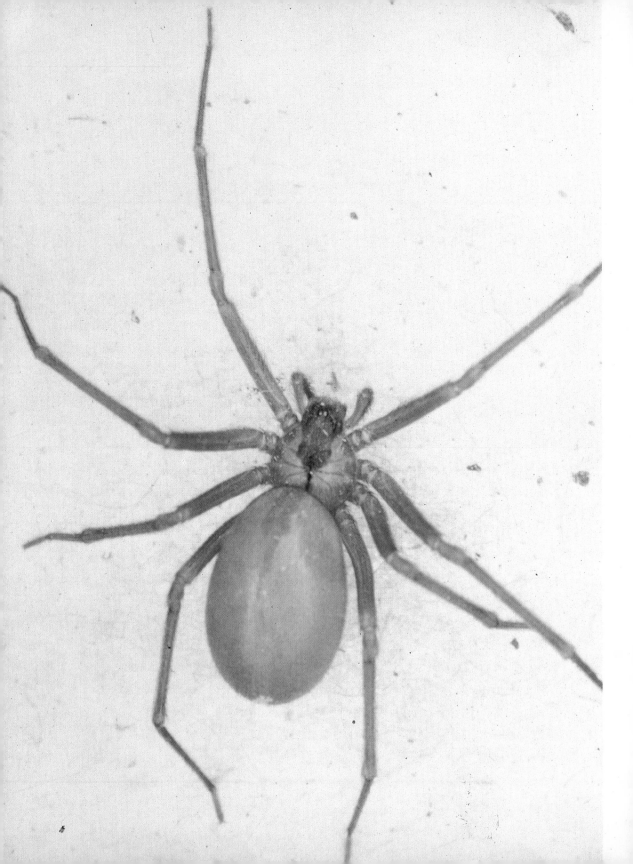

The female recluse spider is slightly smaller than the black widow and the male is almost the same size. Both sexes carry poison and their color varies from a light tan to a dark brown. The brown recluse can be identified by having only six eyes in three pairs and a dark band that stretches from just behind the eyes backward to the end of the cephalothorax in the shape of a violin.

Recluse bites may go unnoticed for hours. Then there may be pain and the bitten area may become numb. The cells around the wound are killed by the venom and slough off, leaving an indented scar. The wound is slow to heal, sometimes taking months. It is important to see a physician at once to get medical help.

Various species of *Lactrodectus*, related to our black widows, are found around the world. Most are small jet-black spiders with beautiful red markings and are poisonous. In nature, striking red coloration may be a warning coloration.

A brown recluse.

# 8

## *Spider Ingenuity*

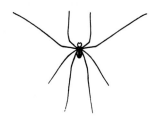

Like most things in this world, whenever we find a hard and fast rule, there is always an exception. This is true about spiders. They are almost always solitary animals, but there are a few species that are gregarious. They build communal webs where a number of spiders live together quite amicably. Such webs are usually found in the tropics. But a few species live in the southern parts of the United States, especially in Florida.

A large web is constructed, covering plants and bushes. Sixty to one hundred spiders may live in such a web, mostly females and immature spiderlings and a few males. The females hang their egg sacs from dry lines in the web. Usually there is a large central nest attached to the nonsticky lines of the web, where many of the spiders go to hide. Social spiders do not attack each other and may join each other in overpowering large insects that bungle into their web.

Aside from the web-weavers, many spiders have developed other uses for their silk. One of the most remarkable is the bolas spider (*Mastophora*). The popular name comes from a weapon invented by the South American Indians and used by cowboys there

A bolas spider, *Mastophora*.

when capturing cattle or wild animals. The bolas has three leather thongs with a stone fastened to each end. The bolas is whirled around and swung at the animal. The beast is brought down in full flight by the bolas twisting around its legs and tripping it.

The spider devised a similar method. To prepare for hunting, she lays several lines of silk along a horizontal tree branch. One of these lines is very loose, so that when the spider crawls to the middle of it, she hangs down well below the branch. She hangs there upside down while she spins out another long line from her spinnerets. At the end of this line, she leaves a big blob of sticky silk. Then she waits. When she senses a flying moth approaching, she begins to swing the line back and forth. It may take her several swings, but before long the sticky end of her line hits the flying moth and the spider can haul in her prey. This spider produces an imitation of the pheromone or perfume that female moths use to attract males.

Other spiders have made variations on this device. One makes a small orb, cuts it loose, and holds it by her legs. When an insect is seen the web is stretched out and dropped over the victim.

Some spiders have gone to such lengths in adapting to their environment that they have changed their shape so that they are almost unrecognizable as spiders. The best way to be sure is to count the legs! Many of these spiders live in the tropics and associate with ants.

Spiders are quick to make use of any advantage that the environment offers. One spider lives in pitcher plants. Since the

Spider on a pitcher plant.

pitcher plant is one of our insect-eating plants, we might consider it an unsafe place for a spider to make its home. The spider spins a tiny shelf, attached to one side of the "pitcher" and waits there. As insects stumble into the trap and fall down the tube, the spider grabs the ones it fancies and eats them. The others it lets go on down to feed the plant. If a dangerous insect like a bee comes down, the spider escapes by letting itself down a long strand of silk. It may even drop into the plant's chemical broth for a few minutes until the danger is past. Its hard outer skin protects it. Then it climbs back up its silken lifeline to its little shelf, where it sits and cleans itself.

Other spiders with original methods of catching prey are spitting spiders. One (*Scytodes thoracica*) is found in some of our northern states in houses. A beautiful whitish spider with black dots, it walks along walls and ceilings of houses at night, looking for small insects. When it sights its prey, it touches it carefully, then gives a convulsive jerk to its body and squirts a sticky gum from its jaws. The victim is stuck and soon entangled. The spider produces this gum from poison glands and squirts it out through the fangs of its jaws.

Spiders are not often associated with water, but some of their activities in that medium are truly remarkable. There is a group of spiders known as the fishing spiders (Pisauridae). They live in damp areas around ponds, lakes, and streams. Such places have many small insects and are very attractive to spiders. These spiders are

Fishing spiders sometimes catch small minnows. Photograph by Harry Ellis.

large but can run across the water on the surface in pursuit of prey and will even dive underwater to catch tiny fish or polliwogs. However, the spiders are so lightweight that they cannot dive very deeply or stay down very long unless they can hold onto some support like a water plant. Otherwise, the air bubbles that cling to the hairs on their legs make them even more buoyant and they pop to the surface like a cork. But they have been timed as long as forty-five minutes underwater.

All of these spiders are quite large, including one that lives in the Okefenokee Swamp in Georgia. Fisher spiders can be found in all states and most of Canada around bodies of still or slow-moving water.

If this seems remarkable, consider the English or European spider that has developed water living to an even greater degree. The water spider (*Argyroneta*) has taken to living underwater and in doing so invented its own little diving bell. She builds her nest underwater and fills it with air which she brings down from the surface. She does this by spinning a strong, thick web, which she fastens to leaves of water plants. Then she swims to the surface, where she tips her abdomen up toward the sky. In doing this, she captures a bubble of air. Holding the bubble close to her body, she dives down to her web and crawls under it. There she releases the air bubble, which rises and pushes the web upward, forming a small air sac.

The water spider spends much of her life inside her water home.

A  European water spider out of the water.

# Index